Usborne
Forgotten Fairy Tales

The Wise
Princess

Retold by Rosie Dickins

Illustrated by Maria Surducan

Reading consultant: Alison Kelly

About
Forgotten Fairy Tales

People have been telling each other fairy tales for thousands of years. Then, a few hundred years ago, collectors began writing the stories down. The ones that became famous were the ones that reflected the ideas of the time.

These stories had patient, polite princesses such as *Snow White* and *Sleeping Beauty*. The tales with bold girls fighting their own battles were ignored.

This series brings to life the stories of those forgotten brave and brilliant girls…

Contents

Chapter 1

The king's test

There was once an old king who lived with his daughters in a crumbling castle.

He loved his daughters very much. "But how do I know if they love ME?" he wondered. In the end, he decided to set them a test.

"Tell me how much you love me!" he said.

"I love you as much as all the world!" said the eldest princess.

"I love you as much as life itself!" said the middle princess.

The king nodded and smiled, delighted with their words.

Greta, the youngest princess, thought for a long time...

"I love you as much as salt," she said simply.

The king frowned.
"Salt is for cooks, not kings!"
he snapped. "Speak again!"

Greta shook her head.

That made the king furious.
"You are not worthy to be a
princess!" he yelled. "Get out –
and don't come back!"

Chapter 2

A cloak of rushes

Greta ran out of the castle.
She ran until her lungs ached
and her heart pounded.

At last, she sank down to
rest on the shore of a lake.
A cold wind rustled the
rushes. She shivered.

Then she had an idea. She picked an armful of rushes and began to weave...

Her fingers worked busily, until she had a stiff, rush cloak. She glanced at her reflection.

Now she looked like a poor country girl or servant.

"I should look for some work," she thought.

A little way off stood a grand house, where an old lord lived.

"I'll try there," she decided.

Chapter 3

The lord's kitchen

*Tap
tap
tap!*

Greta knocked lightly on the back door. A grumpy-looking housekeeper appeared.

"Please, have you any
work?" asked Greta.

"Hmm... well, we do need
someone to wash the dishes."
The housekeeper pointed to a
mountain of greasy pots.

"All right," said Greta, stepping inside. She rolled up her sleeves. Then she rubbed and scrubbed until the pots sparkled and her arms ached.

Meanwhile the housekeeper got on with the cooking. Unfortunately, she hated cooking and it showed.

The first dish the lord ate that night was...

The next was...

Then it got worse...

Ugh, what's THIS?

After dinner, the lord went to bed looking rather green.

Chapter 4

A special soup

The next morning, the lord
did not come downstairs
for breakfast.

"He's sick," said a servant.
"He doesn't want any food."

The lord didn't come
down for lunch either. The
housekeeper sent up a meal,
but it came back untouched.

"I don't know what to do," she sighed. "He just won't eat."

"May I try cooking something?" asked Greta.

The housekeeper nodded.

Greta washed her hands
and began to...

CHOP!

Sizzle!

Stir!

Before long, she had made a
mouth-watering soup.

A servant took up a bowlful.

The lord asked for another
bowlful, and another... and he
began to get better.

In fact, the lord liked the soup so much, he asked Greta to become his cook.

Chapter 5

A royal visit

A few weeks later, the lord held a great banquet.

To His Royal Highness
the King
You are invited to dinner!

"The king himself is coming!"
the housekeeper told Greta.
"The king?" Greta smiled.
"That gives me an idea."

On the day of the
banquet, Greta rose early.
She baked pies and pastries,

and simmered
soups and stews...

...testing and tasting
every dish herself.

"Bring me all the salt," she told the housekeeper. "There must be no mistakes today!"

Servants scurried back and forth, setting the table in the great hall. Then, with a fanfare, the king arrived.

Greta watched from
the shadows.

The first dish was a bowl of steaming soup. The lord tried a spoonful – and frowned.

"It has no taste," he thought.

The king tried his own bowl.
"Pass the salt!" he said.
But there was no salt to
be found.

Next came a rich stew.
The lord took a small bite –
and his heart sank.

The king put down his
spoon. "This needs salt too!"

It was the same with the next dish... and the next.

"I'm s-s-sorry," stammered the lord. "Our food is usually delicious."

The king shook his head
sadly.

"Don't be sorry. It has
helped me to see something
important. I just wish my
daughter Greta was here..."

Greta stepped forward.

I AM here.

The lord gasped.
The king held out his hands
and Greta ran to him.

"Now I see how wise you were," said the king. "I cannot live without salt! Nothing has any taste without it. Will you forgive me?"

Greta nodded, blinking back tears of happiness.

Greta brought out the salt she had hidden and sprinkled it over the food.

Then they sat down to eat together.

Finally salted and served with love, it was the best meal they had ever tasted.

About the story

This story of a wise young princess banished by her father dates back hundreds of years.

In the early 1600s, the famous writer, William Shakespeare, even based part of his play, *King Lear*, on it.

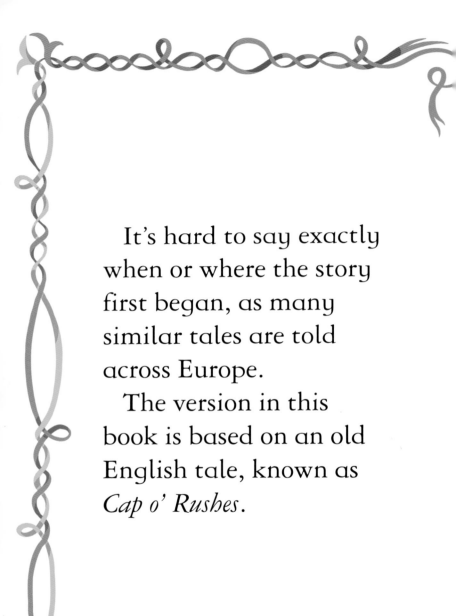

It's hard to say exactly
when or where the story
first began, as many
similar tales are told
across Europe.

The version in this
book is based on an old
English tale, known as
Cap o' Rushes.

Cap O' Rushes

Designed by Laura Bridges
Series designer: Russell Punter
Series editor: Lesley Sims

First published in 2020 by Usborne Publishing Ltd.,
Usborne House, 83-85 Saffron Hill, London EC1N 8RT, England.
usborne.com

St. Julians

18/8/20